Is the Ocean an Animal?

By
Laura Zylinski Batyr

ISBN: 1495298035
ISBN 13: 9781495298035
Library of Congress Control Number: 2014901339
CreateSpace Independent Publishing Platform
North Charleston, South Carolina

For Logan's curiosity about the world,
Sailor's love of bedtime stories,
and Alex's faith in me.

A special thanks to my family,
friends and colleagues for their
support, opinions and editing skills.

A boy and his mother walked over the pebbled driveway and eagerly headed up the familiar beach road—over broken sidewalks—towards the ocean. They both looked forward to these Sunny-Spring afternoons together at the shore.

When they reached the top of the street, they crossed over the boardwalk, kicked off their shoes, and raced each other through the gazebo onto the warm-welcoming sand.

The boy's mother stopped to roll up her pants while watching the boy FLY to the scalloped-receding edge of the ocean.

It wasn't warm enough for the boy to swim, but it was perfect for running away from the chasing waves...screaming with laughter.

The young boy—whose hair looked painted by the sun—turned to his mother and earnestly questioned, after being pursued by another chasing wave, "Mom, is the OCEAN an ANIMAL?"

The question caught his mother by surprise, but after careful thought, she considered that perhaps the ocean was like an animal. The boy's mom replied...

"Sometimes, the ocean is playful and strong like Daddy when he RUNS and ROARS and RACES at you like a bull down the hall to your bedroom."

"Sometimes, the ocean lulls you to sleep like the gentle rocking chair of Grammy's lap and becomes quiet and sleepy like Gramps before his daily nap."

"But sometimes... the ocean can be a GIANT-UGLY-MONSTER that takes the things you treasure the most away—without asking—without giving them back!"

The ocean becomes so ferocious that it knocks our sandcastles down and scars the sand until the next wave comes to rake the ground smooth. Our hard work packing pails and sculpting with shovels disappears much too quickly..."

"But that disappointment will only last until the next wave rolls in..."

"The ocean will spray the air with sea salt... like a fairy sprinkling dust, and the magic of the ocean will lure us back to rebuild our sandcastles (with deeper moats and higher spires) again... and again...and again—until it is time to go home."

The boy stood still, facing the ocean, listening to it breathe in and out, "Shoo-Shaa, Shoo-Shaa, Shoo-Shaa." The ocean sighed and smiled like a dreamy dragon. Its hot breath rolled over the shells and rocks, baking the sand warm.

Seemingly satisfied with his mother's answer, the boy continued to play with the ocean until his mother finally rounded him up for the walk home. The boy ran to the gazebo and sat on the bench, soaking up every last second at the beach, while he waited for his mother to roll down the cuffs of her now sand-filled pants.

Before turning to head back down the familiar beach road, the boy stole one last glance at the ocean, and as he did, the ocean appeared to wink at him with one last breaking wave... reassuring him that the OCEAN was indeed an ANIMAL...and his FRIEND!

Made in the USA
Lexington, KY
21 August 2014